fly me to the moon

Miley Rae Hurley

Sunshine & Moonbeams
Publishing

Perhaps one of the greatest

feelings is that of being loved

deeply, unconditionally, and

fearlessly by another human being.

fly me to the

moon

Miley Rae Hurley

Home

Finding him was

like finding my

way back to a home

I had never

seen before.

It was scary.

It was strange.

But it was wonderful.

Illuminate me

Illuminate me.

Help me shine.

Bring out that light in

me that died out so many

months ago,

because I can't seem to

find it, and you seem to know

just where to look.

Greedy

Lots of girls ask

for flowers and chocolates.

They ask for diamond rings

and sparkly jewelry.

All I really want

is for you to love me

for who I am — for the

person whom I've worked so

hard to become.

For *me.*

(But, hey, I wouldn't complain

about the other stuff, too.)

Willow tree

Just like the weeping willow

by the swampy shore, your

leaves whispered my name.

Your hanging branches reached

out to me hopefully.

Your beautiful bark etching

unmistakable expressions in

your ever-so-slightly swaying
figure.

And there, upon the moss beneath

you, I fell in love with the way

you made me feel, with the way your

beauty graced my eyes, and with the
way

you danced as you called my name.

Butterflies

Oh dear, the butterflies

are loose.

There you went, calling

me beautiful, praising

my accomplishments,

welcoming me into

your life, and there

they fluttered.

Oh dear, you let the

butterflies loose.

Storytime

You wrapped your arm
around me as your parents
told me all about your
childhood, and I do
believe that it just
made me fall harder.

Stealing glances

I can't help

but notice the

way that you

look at me.

How could I not?

It's the look

of someone truly

in love.

Artist

My heart was a blank

canvas before you.

But, there you came,

with your pencils and

your brushes, your paints

and your colors, reviving

the vibrancy that I once

had before it had been

erased by my past hurt.

You brought me

back to life.

Tell me

What do you love?

What do you hate?

Where do you love to go?

What do you love to do?

Favorite animal?

Favorite food?

Favorite game?

Tell me your dreams.

Tell me your fears.

Tell me random facts you know.

Tell me anything, just tell me

about you because I would love

to know so much about you.

Windows

They say eyes are windows
to the soul, and they
are, because in yours, I
see the world.

Superman

Please just come and sweep

me off my feet. Save me from

the clutches of evil.

Oh, wait.

You already have.

I love you

I love you more than summer.

I love you more than art.

I love you more than music.

I love you more than dinosaurs.

I love you more than anything else
that I catch myself nerding-out
over, which is huge considering
I've continued to love the same
things for years and years.

Then you came along, and
you're new.

But you're wonderful.

Philosophy

Sometimes, I think writing a book is more difficult than writing a song. Coming up with an effective way to make a reader thoroughly enjoy what they're reading isn't easy when you don't have a melody to aid them through. However, on the contrary, songwriting can be difficult, too. How do you come up with that catchy tune that will draw listeners in? How do you write rhythmic words that people might relate to if they listen hard enough? The whole idea of writing, no matter what it is or how it's done, is just one big puzzle. You just have to figure out *what* pieces fit *where*. More than that, people tend to favor words that *speak* to them, rather than the words that *listen*. They like the melody. They like when things are straightforward, like songs. When they're asked to pull their own emotions from their life to relate to what they're reading, they get uncomfortable. They run, and they give up on the text.

When I found you, you stayed, and you read the words that *listened*.

Paris

Your eyes sparkle like

the Eiffel Tower at dusk.

My, how I've always

wanted to go to Paris.

Tidal wave

Every affectionate feeling

that I've ever had for you

crashes over me like a

tidal wave every time I

lay my gentle eyes on you.

Can we?

Can I stay awhile?

Can I be with you?

Can we just be *us*?

No rules.

No expectations.

Just. Us.

Us and however much

time we have left.

Heart

My heart jumps for joy

whenever I see your

name on my phone.

I don't know

There's something about the way your
nose

scrunches when you smile or laugh.

   I don't know, it gives me butterflies.

There's something about the way you

open doors for me and take me on dates.

   I don't know, it makes me feel wanted.

There's even something about the way

you say "I love you."

   I don't know, but I know you mean it.

I think it's love, but then again, I

don't know, and I can't quite

put my finger on it yet.

Rubber band

I used to wear this hair tie around
my wrist, so whenever I was feeling
anxious, I would pull it back and
watch it snap into place.

When I met you, and I saw how
gently you smiled and how lovingly
you'd caressed my rosy cheek in
your palm, it finally put me at
ease enough to make me leave the
hair tie resting on my desk.

Memories

Sometimes I just wish I

could put all my old memories

from past relationships in a

folder and shut it tight to

make room for ours that we have

yet to make together.

Fairy lights

The stringed fairy lights

dangling from my canopied

bed remind me of all the

beautiful little impacts that

you've had on my life.

Push

My heart has been

pushed,

shoved, and

thrown

past boundaries I

didn't even know

that I had.

It's thrilling,

and I love it.

Rare

I've never met anyone

as similarly bonded and

singularly affectionate

in such an open, shameless

manner as you.

Thank you for not

being ashamed to show

me that you love me.

Color theory

Certain colors go with each other,
and certain colors do not.

Certain people go with each other,
and certain people do not.

If we were colors, our hues and
our shades would match and blend
together perfectly in such unison,
you'd think you were looking at
something as beautiful as a sunset
and as rich and as vibrant as
thriving jungle flowers.

Attached

I am not being clingy. I am simply

embracing the fact that life has

given me the chance to love

someone unconditionally and that,

I feel, is the greatest gift.

Highway

Let my hands be the

highway to my soul,

and let my eyes have

the power to guide

you there.

Mistakes

The worst thing a person

can do is fail to tell someone

just how much they love them

before they are no longer able to.

Love song

Since I don't actually
know how to write a love
song, let this book be
my love song to you.

Stealing glances

One time, I caught you

searching for me among

throngs of people. I had

found you before you found

me, and I could've sworn

I saw your eyes light up

when you finally did.

Mountains

All the mountains I've had to

climb to find you were worth it.

Stars

When I look to my future,

I no longer see darkness.

I see fireflies.

I see sunrises.

I see stars.

Always

You tell me your scared of failure.
That you're scared of going out on
your own and messing up somehow —
not succeeding at the career that
you dreamed of or not ending up
where you wish to be. I am, too,
but that's part of life. Risking
your comfort and your security to
seek out the things you want most.
That's what makes life such a
thrill.

So fall. Stumble. Fail. Get up, and
try again. If you fall, fall into
my arms because I will always be
there to catch you. If you stumble,
I will be the balance that you need
to regain your stability. If you
fail, do it with the confidence of
someone who is proud of themself
for even giving it a shot.

Letting you fail will never be
something I could accomplish.

Handsome boy

You will always

be the

(cutest)

(loveliest)

(sweetest)

(gentlest)

(kindest)

(prettiest)

best boy to me.

Safe and sound

In your arms,

I feel *safe.*

I feel *secure.*

I feel *sound.*

Apart

I even hate hanging up

phone calls with you.

Overjoyed

No one has ever made me

laugh so easily.

No one has ever been able

to cheer me up so quickly

the way that you do.

The sad part is that you

don't even have to try.

Not sad for you, sad for

those before that tried.

Time

I don't care that we have limited
hours.

I don't care that anything I do
from now until the day I die will
eventually be forgotten through the
simple passage of time.

I don't care that, despite all of
my efforts to be well-known and
loved, I can't be good enough for
everyone.

What I do care about is that right
now, in this moment, I love you.
Nothing is going to change that.
Nothing is going to tear that
apart. Time doesn't scare me. The
end of the world doesn't scare me.
I am going to love you until my
body gives out.

Until my lungs collapse.

Until the very last

beat of my heart.

Necklace

He makes me long for his initial

to hang around my neck.

The movies

Why is it that now every time

I watch one of those corny romance

movies, I can't help but wish it

was him and I?

Stuff of fiction

I only ever believed that

this kind of love existed

in the works of fiction.

Tattoo

You asked me if I

want any tattoos when

we get older.

I told you I do.

I want your love

tattooed in an arrow

shape on my heart.

Moth

Like a moth to flame, I

am drawn to your love.

Pretty

One thing that I love about you

is that you make me feel like the

most beautiful girl in the world,

even when I most definitely am not.

Come sail away

You sailed onto my rocky shore,

anchoring your ship to my

harbor, bearing my great load

with ease atop your prominent

stern and never faltering

under the weight of it all.

You withstood the cargo

that came with the cost

of having my heart, and

despite knowing how heavy

it was, you never decided

to sail anywhere else.

Doubt

Don't ever

doubt my love

for you, for

you will

continue

to be sorely

incorrect

in your

assumptions.

Je t'aime

Bonjour.

Enchanté.

Tu m'aimes?

Clever

If I had a dollar for every time you've

told me one of your corny, ridiculously

adorable pick-up lines that you use

to make me smile, I'd be rich.

Listen

Shh.

Listen, now.

Do you hear that?

No?

Listen again.

It's the sound of

my insistent heartbeat

slowing and relaxing

from the peace that

you bring my soul.

100 years

When you're in love, and you think about

how much time you have on Earth,
100 years

just doesn't seem like long enough.

Name

What is even the purpose

of my legal name when I just

like the ones you give me more?

Battle scars

Come and heal my

torn limbs.

My broken soul.

My fractured heart.

Come and make them

whole again.

Make *me* whole again.

Travel

Traveling the world.

Exploring gorgeous places.

Studying exotic plants and animals.

Learning about new cultures.

All of these things I

have wanted very badly in

my life, and now, perhaps

I have someone to splendidly

share my passions with.

Growing up

What if our lives don't turn out
the way that we planned?

What if it's all just downhill
from here on out?

If growing up and getting older
are the scariest things I will
ever have to do in my life, then
I'm perfectly fine with that,
because that would mean never
having to give my heart
to someone other than you.

Intertwined

Can our hands stay

Intertwined forever?

Can our hearts just remain

forever entangled in this

beautiful synchronization

of two souls who just want

to be seen with one another?

Known for never being

seen one without the other?

Known for completing the

other in graceful dance rather

than one-sided dependency?

Worry

My parents always told me that I
needed to find someone who would
help me thrive and achieve my
dreams. Someone who I don't have to
lean on all the time, but, rather,
only when necessary. Someone who
will rise with me instead of
watching me rise and sitting in the
shadows of my glory.

He isn't any of the things that my
parents warned me about. *He* is the
person they *encouraged* me to find.
He is my sun when the sun isn't
shining. He clears the fog from my
clouded mind. He gives me gentle
nudges when I am too scared to
start things on my own.

He is supportive, loving,
encouraging, and I couldn't ask for
anyone else to get me through this
crazy, chaotic, wonderful life.

Seen

I don't see you as a perfect
person. I don't think that you
can't do anything wrong. Love
hasn't blinded me from the fact
that you're human. Love has opened
my eyes and helped me see *you*. The
real you. The *you* that you might
try to hide from others.

You are flawed. You make mistakes.
You mess up. You fall. You hurt
people without meaning to. You cry.
You get angry. You feel like giving
up when life just gets too heavy to
bear. You have regrets. You will
continue to make errors in your
life for as long as you'll live,
and I, in loving you the way that I
do, will see, not past, but *through*
each and every thing.

Our flaws don't define us, but they
do contribute to the person we
become, and I love the person that
you turned out to be.

Pure imagination

Never in my wildest of dreams

would I have ever pictured

finding someone like you.

5th street

The street where we had

our very first chat.

The street where we had

our very first date.

The street where everything

sparked new flames,

setting off more fireworks

than our town's annual

4th of July celebration.

Hold me

I still remember

this one night

at your house.

I started crying,

and before you

even knew why, you

wrapped your

solid, outstretched

arms around me,

holding me close

and letting me cry

on your shoulder.

Athlete

You don't need to

be in a sport for

me to love you.

~~Baseball.~~

~~Basketball.~~

~~Football.~~

~~Tennis.~~

~~Soccer.~~

~~Wrestling.~~

It seems to be a standard

nowadays, but I couldn't

care less about it.

I miss you

In every room that I walk into,
noticing

that you aren't in there, my heart

aches from the thought of you.

Blanket

Like a blanket in the cold,

a cabin in the dead of winter,

or a fire in the darkness,

you shroud me with such

love that anyone would

consider themself lucky

to ever behold within

their gracious soul.

Guitar

I got a guitar recently.

An acoustic one.

I catch myself learning

mostly love songs.

Funny that they all

make me think of you.

Perhaps I should try

to write you one?

Hoodie

Could I have

one of your

hoodies, please?

I'll wear it

when I'm

sad.

happy.

annoyed.

angry.

tired.

Basically, all

of the time.

But it smells

like you, so.

Author

If I write our story down, will you make sure it never ends?

Ring

My entire life of hurt fluttered

before my very eyes like a picture
book

of memories the minute you slipped

the glittering ring from my

middle finger and placed it

gently upon the finger meant

for wedding bands.

Diamonds

Diamonds are, in fact,

not a girl's best friend.

Most can't even get

themself a diamond.

What *is* a girl's best

friend is a boy who

truly loves a girl.

Those boys are diamonds.

Watchdog

You told me you were allergic

to certain types of food, and

I suddenly found myself aware

of everything that I brought

near you and that others offered

up for you to eat, despite

the fact that I had never

even considered it before.

Silence

I used to hate the quiet.

Now, I appreciate it more.

It gives me more time

alone with my thoughts

and much more time to

think about you.

Spark

I had recently lost my passion for
drawing and creating art. Over the
years, it just...

...faded...vanished.

Then you came along. Funny enough, the
very first time I met your parents,
they gifted me an entire art case that
you never used as a child. It was in
pristine condition — the paints and
colored pencils looked like they hadn't
even been touched.

I still had traces of my creativity
from before, so I decided to draw you a
picture and color it using the supplies
you gave me. You've always loved
dinosaurs, so that is what I drew.

It turned out to be the best drawing
I'd ever made, even though I hadn't
drawn anything in over six months.

You got me my spark back.

Birds of a feather

I'm tired of flying solo.

Please, fly me to the moon.

Fly me to mars.

Fly me anywhere, but please

don't let me fly by myself.

Halley's comet

Soulmates only come

around once in one

person's lifetime.

Typically, so does

Halley's comet.

Tide

Let the tide wash over me,

cleansing my body, my mind,

and my soul while your

loving currents draw me

into the warmest embrace.

Locket

I've never had

much interest in

wearing a locket,

but now, I ache for

one with your picture

waiting for me inside.

Riverbank

Easing through the flowing stream, I rest myself upon the large, smooth rocks, their solid bodies providing me comfort. I reach my hand out, my fingertips brushing the surface of the crystal-clear water. A minnow swims by. Cattails rustle on the graveled shore. I can feel the sand beneath my bare feet. My face illuminated by the sunshine smiling down on my face through the canopy from above. This creek that I walked so often when I was young now reminding me only of the things that are dear to me.

My parents.

My friends.

You.

If you would like, you can sit with me. Here, on this gorgeous afternoon. Stay awhile. We'll tell each other stories, and we'll make each other laugh.

Be like this stream and keep reminding me of the things that matter.

Miracle

He looks so divine in the light from this streetlamp, like he was gifted to me from the most breathtaking place you could possibly imagine.

Request

Was it so much to ask

to have somebody

that I can spoil

with everything

that I have?

If someone means

that world to you,

you should show

it to them.

Don't just use

your words and

tell them.

Archer

How did cupid's

arrow manage

to find the

one weak spot

in my frozen,

bitter heart?

Surname

I really like the way your

last name looks when I write

it next to my first name.

Automatic

My smile is simply

automatic the second

I get a glimpse of

your sweet face.

Pity

I feel such sadness for animals

who don't mate for life and

for humans who never find

happiness with the person

that they end up with.

How sorrowful would it be

to never find that joy?

Thrill me

Take me on the most

dangerous, exciting,

frightening,

blood-pumping,

adrenaline-inducing

adventures of my life.

Make me wonder if

I'll live to next

week because of the

risk of it all.

I'm giving you

permission to

thrill me.

Fly me to the moon

Plant your flag upon the soil of my
heart.

Claim your territory on the barren,
vast stretches of my soul.

Muck up my orbit with your boot prints
along my many craters.

I've been struck by asteroids. I've
faced intrusion across my surface.
People have come along and stomped on
my beautiful flowers that took so long
to bloom. I am a planet full of
mistakes, blemishes, and imperfections.

And yet, when I find myself trapped
within my dark side, you offer to fly
me to another moon. Another planet.
Another galaxy.

Just to relieve me from the pain.

Crush

You're the first person I've had a

crush on where I didn't feel immensely

jittery around you, and that isn't a

bad thing, either.

It means, to me, that there is
something

there that makes me think we can last.

It's not like I don't get butterflies

around you, but they aren't so much

of a constant thing. Sometimes, they

flutter their wings every now and then
to

remind me that they are still here with
me.

There is security in knowing that my

feelings for you won't fade, because

butterflies don't live forever.

Car crash

Every person I've been with,

I have swerved into ditches to

avoid the red flags that were

leaping out at me everywhere.

I've drifted into snowbanks.

I've rolled top over bottom across

the dirty, icy pavement because

I saw something that scared me.

With you, I've managed to

remain safely on the road.

Storm dance

I don't care if it's raining —
would

you still dance in the rain with
me?

Love

Love fearlessly.

Love passionately.

Love truthfully.

Whatever you do, *love*.

We only have one life

on this earth, and

you don't want to

spend it drowning

in the guilt of

your refusal to

love someone.

16 years

Our birthdays are only two weeks apart.

Hard to believe we are already 16,
right?

Now, we can drive. We'll have to start

considering colleges sooner than we'd
like.

Some people will dismiss what we have

for merely being "young love."

Which it is, I suppose.

But maybe they don't understand what

successful, healthy love is supposed

to look like at our age, because
they've

just had bad experiences with it.

Risk

Will you take a

chance on me?

On *us?*

Because I would

risk it all.

Quick

It's unsettling how soon

I realized I truly

loved you when we had

barely started dating.

Looking glass

Sometimes, my life with

you just feels so

unreal that I fool

myself into thinking

I'm staring at some

alternate reality of

myself through a

looking glass.

Caught in the moment

On our first date, I caught
the faintest glimpse of your
soul within your starry eyes,
and from that moment on,
I knew my life would
never be the same.

Telescopic

I'm starting to misremember when

we first met, because I feel

like I've known you for a lifetime.

Sunshine

Your love

feels like

the warm

summer sun

that shines

down on our

midwestern

hometown.

Stardust

Within all of the

nebulas in all of the

galaxies in the universe,

and within all of the

clusters of stars and

rocks floating in space,

however many there may be,

I happened to be raised

and growing up in the one

town that both of us

call home on the same

massive floating rock

that sprouted our lives

in the first place.

Sunset

Your eyes remind me of trees illuminated

by the cast of golden light from sunsets.

With the sun behind them, they glow with

this brownish tint that adds the richest

hues to the brightest of phenomena.

Rollercoaster

You know, I've never been on a
rollercoaster before. I don't know why.
I either haven't had the chance or have
been too scared to go near one.

Can we go someday? Just you and me?
Maybe some of our friends?

I want to walk through the blistering
sun with you in the summer. I want to
be so scared to go on certain rides
that only through your convincing can
you encourage me to change my mind. I
want to frantically reach for your arm
or your hand, something to hold onto
for when we reach that terrifying drop.
I want to indulge in incredibly
unhealthy fair food with you, but I'd
steer you away from the peanuts because
they'll make you sick.

Let's go. I'll drive.

Friend

Not only did I find, in him, the
love of

my life, but I also found my best
friend.

Skills

You may have the advantage in

pool, but I absolutely demolish

you in UNO.

I just wanted to say that,

it makes me laugh every time.

Terms & conditions

As with most things, I also come
with an absurdly long list of
rules and requirements.

Most just scroll through, not
even bothering to care about what
it says or what anything means.

They press "Agree" and move on.

Those contracts all fell
through, by the way.

But you...I actually *saw* you take
it all in, accept me for who I was,
and continue to stick around.

Promise

Look me in the

eyes and promise

me that you

understand

just how much

I love you.

Curlique

Every chance we have together,

I can't resist playing with the

little tufts of hair that hang

over your forehead like overgrown

vines with their wispy arms

and dancing leaves.

I call them your Superman curls.

Atlas

Adorn me with your

broken wings, and

make me bear the

weight of your

life's burdens,

for I will teach

you how to fly, and

I would carry the

entire world on

my back for you.

Poet

You don't need

to be a poet to

write about how

much you love

someone.

All you need to

be is nothing more

than yourself —

a human being.

Heal

We've both been hurt before. We've both
been through breakups. Some worse than
others. We've both given our hearts to
others who've just ended up closing
their fists around them. We've been
thrown to the side, pushed around, let
down. We've been broken. We've cried.
We've felt so much rage in our bodies
that you just can't help but shake with
anger over the fact that some people
just aren't meant to stick around, and
there isn't anything to be done to
change that. The world hasn't been
particularly kind to either of us, and
that's okay. It's not about what has
happened to us. It's about what *will*
happen. The things we can control — on
our own and as a team.

Maybe we could be the healing that both
of us need every once and awhile? When
life pushes you down and laughs in your
face while your scraped knee is
bleeding down your leg. When it thinks
your dreams are nothing but silly
wishes that you thought of as a kid.

Life, the world, and cruel people don't
have anything on us as long as we don't
give up on each other like the others
did.

Different

I like the change that I'm

seeing in myself.

I look so much better

now, *happier,* than I did

about four months ago.

I laugh louder.

Smile wider.

Love deeper.

Appreciate *more.*

Hmph.

I wonder why.

Perfection

Somehow, despite all the

far better things you could've

complimented me on, you managed

to compliment me on parts of

myself that I had always

been so insecure about.

Your legs are perfect.
Your hair is so pretty.
You look beautiful.

Thank you, truly,

because without those

little comments that you

don't think mean a lot,

I'd still be insecure

about those very things.

Oblivion

I'm more scared of losing you than I

am of oblivion itself and the

nothingness that resides within it.

Would I be me?

I wonder...would I be

the writer — the poet — that

I am today if I hadn't

been hurt by others before

who've claimed to love me?

To love someone is to turn

your pain into something that

you can grow from and thrive on.

My writing *is* my pain.

Is and *was.*

It is also my truest display

of my undying affection.

Comparison

Their love was hardly *love*

in comparison to yours.

Rest

Come.

Rest your tired,

weary soul upon

the cushioned fabric

of my heart.

Let me hold you

until you forget your

troubles and realize

that nothing can hurt

you if you just believe

in my love for you.

Author's Note

Yes, I'm young. No, I don't have a lot of life experience yet. However, that doesn't mean that every poem that I wrote about loving someone doesn't matter.

Young love might sound impossible. It might sound like something that could never be real. After all, people like to think that young people aren't old enough to understand things like that.

If you're young, and reading this book made you think of a certain someone in your life that, perhaps, you love like crazy, then don't be ashamed of it. Love is one of the most powerful emotions and, when withheld from those we love, it can wreak havoc on the souls of those caught in the crossfire of denial.

Don't let people tell you that you're too young to be in love. Don't let anyone tell you that you shouldn't express your emotions towards someone.

Love is too beautiful a light to simply snuff it out.

Acknowledgements

The entirety of this book took me a month to write. It's crazy. I didn't get the motivation from nowhere, though. The people in my life and all the encouragement they've given me gave me the drive that I needed to push through challenges and standstills to reach the official publishing of my second book. Hopefully, my second of many. ☺

I will never stop thanking my parents, Teresa and William Hurley. These two are the best people I know. They've never given up on me, even when times have felt utterly hopeless. They were the key to this book, really. They were the ones who taught me how to love as deeply as I do. I love you guys so very much.

Thank you to my beta readers, yet again, for making sure everything looks good. Paisley Fellers, Emmalyn Splitter, and Malina Luckhart. You girls are some of the greatest friends

I have ever had in my life. I love you guys.

One of the biggest thank-yous must go to my extremely talented aunt Tonya Wells. She took the photo for my "About the Author" page, and it turned out amazing. Her business is Tonya Wells Portraits at Poetic Grace & Co. Portrait Studio in Fairbury, Illinois. It is one of the best photography studios I have ever seen. I love you, and you're definitely my favorite photographer.

About the Author

Miley Rae Hurley is a new author who, as of 2024, published her first book and has now published her second within a five-month period. She has been working hard for several years to fight through procrastination, self-doubt, and writer's block to finally reach her huge dream of being an officially published author. The goal of her writing is to show people that they are not alone. She implores them to know that emotions *should* be felt, not ignored. Writing has always been one of her favorite pastimes. She adores expressing herself through the use of similes, metaphors, and detailed descriptions of emotions. She wants her readers to feel her pain through her words. She wants her words to bleed every drop of passion that she pours into her writing. Whenever she gets the chance, she is reading new books to expand her extensive vocabulary, and when she's not reading, she's either creating art or making new memories with her friends that she adores so dearly. She is incredibly grateful for everything she has worked so hard for. Stay tuned for more works by her if you enjoyed what you read.